WHEN LOVE COMES TO TOWN

CALLIE GARDNER

Email: calliegardnerbooks@gmail.com

Callie Gardner's Newsletter

If you love reading sweet, clean, Western Romance stories why not join Callie Gardner's newsletter and receive advance notification of new releases and more!

Simply sign up here: http://eepurl.com/cJoqqb

And get your *FREE* copy of **Maggie's Education**

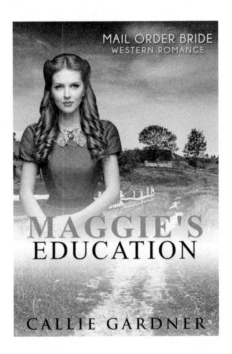

CHAPTER 1

*A*lysse Elizabeth Rearden tapped her foot as she stood in the shadow of the station, she watched as the other passengers milled around the platform. She hadn't travelled in this capacity before, but had she known it would be this entertaining, she might have chosen to in the past.

There were all sorts of people to watch, from the lowliest of Savannah's residents to those that moved in the highest circles of polite society. Some she recognized and while there had been a time where she would have engaged them in conversation, she would not do so now.

As if they would even converse with her anyway.

Alysse shifted her weight to the other foot, clad in a fashionable calf leather boot, dyed to match her forest green traveling habit. The habit was made of soft wool, keeping her warm in the unusually cold weather that had descended over the southern city today. It was the middle of summer, yet, because of recent rain, it felt more like fall.

"Look. There she is. I wonder where she is going?"

A feminine giggle followed the question. "Likely to hide her face. I can't believe she has stayed in this area so long!"

Alysse's shoulders stiffened at the whisperings behind her,

refusing to turn around and face the gossipers. She was used to it by now, after suffering for nearly a year under this city's scrutiny. There had been a time, oh what a time, when her family was one of the premier families in this city and their daughter, Alysse had enjoyed the finer things in life, from the finest clothing to a dizzy array of parties, balls and social gatherings. She had attended the prestigious finishing school for fine young ladies, and nearly a year to the date, had captured the eye of Stephen Filmort. Stephen was the only son of another prominent family, their wealth stemmed from the trading of goods on the Savannah River.

When he proposed marriage, her family and his had been elated and Alysse had thrown herself into planning the finest wedding that Savannah society would see in a year's time.

Except now, she was standing on the platform, awaiting the train that would take her away from the city permanently.

Blowing out a breath, Alysse fought the urge to seat herself on the bench in front of the depot station, keeping her shoulders aligned with her back, as she had been taught. It would have been perhaps easy to have left when the scandal first broke, but she had held out hope that it was not true, that somehow, they had gotten it all wrong and her father was not the leader in the scheme that had swindled thousands out of their money.

But alas, it hadn't been a mistake nor a bad dream. Her father, once a well-respected banker, was in fact the man they had accused and thrown in prison. Alysse and her mother had gone from being accepted into polite society to finding those doors shut tightly on them. Stephen had broken off their engagement and little by little, their home and belongings were sold out from under them. She and her mother had barely escaped with their clothes, moving into a home of a sympathizer for a few months to tide them over.

Alysse had attempted to move on with her life, but she hadn't realized that a reputation was such a fickle thing. None of her friends, not even Stephen would even converse with her, going as far as to walk on the opposite side of the street whenever she would see them. The horrid newspaper ran her father's story for weeks on end, detailing their ruin for all to see. While their sympathizer had allowed them a place to gather their wits about them and a new plan for their lives, it wasn't meant to be a permanent solution.

And then, well, the worst happened. Alysse's mother, stricken by the fact that she was no longer the well to do lady that she had once been, took a fair amount of opium one evening and never woke up. Alysse had been devastated but also angry that she had abandoned her daughter when she needed her the most.

Now, with no family or friends willing to support her any longer, Alysse had done the unthinkable.

She had accepted an advertisement for a mail order bride. She had no funds, save the few bills from pawning the last bit of her mother's belongings, no future in this city. She was an outcast, destined to become a fallen woman if she wished to eat and have a roof over her head.

She would not stoop that low. Her pride would not allow it.

The train sounded in the distance and people hurriedly cleared the tracks, the bellow of smoke growing closer. Truthfully, Alysse did not wish to leave her city. This was where she had been raised. This was all she knew.

But she knew she had to. There was nothing left for her here and it was up to her to move forward and bring some pride back to the Rearden name.

Even if she wouldn't hold it for much longer. In a few short days, she would be married to a stranger, one that had accepted her letter without question. She would become his wife, share a home and a bed with him. Not only that, she would live in a dusty town in Texas, forever remembering this life that had slipped through her fingers.

As the train grew closer, Alysse pasted a smile on her face, holding her valise in front of her. Above all, she was a lady in every sense of the word. She would continue to be that lady no matter what she faced in her new home. Her mother would want her to do so.

And she would not be afraid. Not even in the slightest.

For if she showed fear, that would be a weakness and Rearden's did not show weakness, did they?

CHAPTER 2

*R*obert Chastain looked at the tallied numbers on the sheet of paper, frowning as he saw the total. It was barely enough to run the hotel for another week, let alone a month or two. What had happened to this one flourishing town?

He laid down his pencil and ran a hand through his hair, looking out over the barren lobby of the Lucky Star Hotel. The building itself was deathly silent, the warm summer wind rattling the shutters, reminding Robert that he had to nail them down once more before winter set in.

But the shutters were the least of his concerns. The roof needed patching and the once fine linen was starting to show its wear in each room above his head. The entire place needed a good dusting, but Robert had no funds to hire anybody to clean.

Not that it mattered. There were no guests to fill the rooms anyway.

Robert picked up his pencil once more, looking over the list of items he needed to purchase from the mercantile, crossing off the ones that he could live without for another month. When he had returned to Harriston, Texas, this was not what he had imagined he would find. For four years, he had spent his time in California, attempting to find the gold that would make him a wealthy man. He had sifted more soil than he cared to remember, until his back ached, and his hands cramped from holding the pan.

But his hard work had paid off. While the gold he found hadn't made him a wealthy man, it had provided more than enough to come back to his hometown and resurrect his family's hotel. His uncle had run it for many years, but had died a year ago, therefore giving Robert a reason to halt his gold mining and come back to the town he had grown up in. The small amount of funds he had collected in California had worked for a time, allowing him to not worry too much about the lack of guests that hadn't filled his book.

But now, that money was nearly all gone.

Robert stepped from behind the counter and placed his hands in his pockets as he walked from the lobby to the unfinished section of restaurant he had envisioned, the tables still covered with white cloths, that were somewhat dusty. One of his main reasons for taking over the hotel was to open a fine restaurant, one that would carry on his family's name for generations. Like every Chastain before him, he had learned every skill that went into running a hotel, including how to cook simple meals. Over the years, Robert had developed his skills into something he believed would be worthwhile for this hotel.

If only he could afford it.

The bell tinkled over the door and he hurried back to the lobby, finding a portly man with a valise waiting at the counter. "Welcome to the Lucky Star," Robert breathed. It was a customer!

"'Tis a fine hotel," the customer said, placing his valise on the counter. "Very fine."

"Thank you," Robert said, wincing as dust floated up from the page that he turned in the guestbook. If the man noticed, he didn't say anything, but gave Robert a broad smile. "Can I get you a room sir?"

"One room, yes," the man replied, tapping his valise. "But I have another proposition for you as well sir. I am in need of a large space to hold a party of sorts in a few days and your hotel looks to be just what I am looking for."

A thrill shot through Robert. A party? That would mean more

guests which in turn meant more money. It was exactly what he needed to happen.

Someone was smiling down on him today! "Of course, sir. I have a fine restaurant that you may use for your party."

"Good, good," the man said, extending his hand. "James Loudon at your service."

Robert shook the man's hand. "Robert Chastain."

James grinned as he released Robert's hand, opening his valise. "I will be willing to pay of course, for your space." Robert watched with bated breath as the gentleman pulled out some bills, placing them on the counter. It was far more than Robert would have imagined seeing, his mind already whirling with possibilities. With these funds, he could open the restaurant, at least temporarily. "Is this enough?"

Robert's grin was genuine as he looked at James. "More than enough." Someone had answered his prayers. "Thank you very much, sir."

James shook his head, picking up his valise. "No, thank *you*. I am just fortunate to find this place for my party. I trust you can provide additional lodging if need be?"

Robert chuckled. "Of course. Let me retrieve your key and I will show you to your room." He turned away from the counter, his hands trembling lightly as he retrieved one of the keys from the cubby hole behind him. Whatever he had done to have this chance, he was grateful. This could be the start of the future he had hoped for, a chance to carry on the family traditions and make his relatives proud.

Most of all, he wouldn't have to shut down the family hotel.

CHAPTER 3

$\mathcal{T}$hree Days Later…

"And furthermore, this heat is stifling. Stifling I tell you! I detest sweating. Ladies should not sweat. It's utterly disgusting."

Alysse was only half listening to the woman to her left, clenching her hands in her lap to keep from putting her hand over the woman's mouth. Desiree was her name and she had gotten into the coach the same time Alysse had, unable to take the train to their destination. Desiree was from Boston, where apparently women never perspired.

Alysse, on the other hand, could feel the wetness of her own perspiration seeping through the many layers of clothing she wore on her back, her palms sweaty from gripping them so tightly together for the better part of the morning. Riding the stagecoach had been miserable to say the least, and not because of Desiree's constant conversation. She felt every bump in the road, her body jarring as the wheels ran over the ruts and longed for the comfort of the train once more. At least she had her own bench, not having to share the space with anyone else.

Across from her and Desiree was another woman, her dress threadbare, her boots scuffed and worn. She looked nervous and while Desiree had attempted to learn her name, the woman clearly wasn't interested in making new friends. Alysse felt a bit sorry for the woman. Though she had fallen on hard times, she hadn't suffered real poverty yet.

The stagecoach hit another rut and Alysse bounced on the hard leather seat, knowing she would have bruises all over her body by the morning.

They had to be close to Harriston.

"Do you think they dance in this town?" Desiree said, a wistful look on her face. "I hope that they do. I love dancing."

The young woman across the coach snorted but quickly covered it up with a cough, causing Desiree's lips to flatten. Alysse fought the urge to laugh herself. She would be grateful when they did arrive to their new home.

Fortunately, it was not long before the coach slowed, and all the women did a collective sigh. Alysse felt the nervousness start to build as the wooden buildings started to pass by the window. What would her husband look like? What would he think of her? All she knew about him was that his name was Nelson and that he was looking for a refined wife to join him and bring some class to the small town. He was to meet her in front of the general store, wearing a brown coat and Alysse could not wait to meet the man that was to help her turn her life around. After so much disappointment in her life, she was looking forward to something positive happening.

The coach shuddered to a stop and the worn woman hurried out of the door. "Eager to meet her family," Desiree muttered as Alysse accepted the hand of the driver and climbed out of the coach herself. Her traveling gown was hopelessly wrinkled, and she was in need of a cool bath, but that would have to wait.

Looking about the town, she could only hope that her new husband was part of something grander than what she was seeing. It was dusty, very dusty, with no real street as she was used to the cobblestones of Savannah. There were no structures other than tired looking wooden outbuildings, their signs swinging in the warm breeze.

Where was she at?

Looking at the driver, she gave him her best smile. "Would you watch over my things? I am to meet my husband at the mercantile."

He tipped his hat. "Of course, ma'am. I will make sure that no one bothers them."

"Very much appreciated kind sir," she said and smiled. The one good thing was that no one was looking at her in disdain, whispering behind her back. No one knew of her father's ruin here, nor did they see anything other than a well to do woman in a fine gown. This was going to work. She would make sure that it did.

Alysse made her way to the store, frowning as she saw a gaggle of women standing there, including the two others from the coach. A man stepped out of the crowd and she breathed a sigh of relief at his tall form, noting the brown coat. This was Nelson, her intended. He was handsome enough, his smile warm and friendly and picked up her skirts as he noted her, holding up his hand in welcome.

"Dearest Alysse," he said, holding out his hands towards her. "You have arrived. Good. If you will follow me."

"But what about us?" Desiree stated. "Who is she?"

Nelson held up his hand, calming the crowd. "Ladies, I will explain everything to you all if you will just please come with me. I have cold lemonade waiting for you."

She could use a cool refreshment right about now. "Nelson, if I can have a moment."

Nelson gave her another smile. "I must have you follow me Alysse, please."

Frowning at his sudden dismissal, Alysse fell in step with the rest of the women as Nelson led them down a side alley, the smell of urine and refuse strong in the air that caused her to wish she had her rose scented handkerchief pressed against her face.

Soon, they were herded into a building, the stale air offering no relief from the heat outside. "In here ladies," Nelson announced, moving them into a room that resembled a dining room. The tables were gleaming in the sunlight that was streaming through the windows and Alysse made sure to keep herself ahead of the crowd, a pleasant smile on her face. She had no idea what was going on, but she would keep herself in Nelson's direct gaze so that he would see her. Perhaps these women were here to witness their wedding.

Nelson closed the doors and held up his hands, commanding attention of the room. "I know you all must have many questions. I am the gentleman that wrote the advertisement, but I answered each and every one of yours with the best of intentions."

"Are you gonna marry all of us then?" Desiree asked, her hands on her hips. "Because I came here to get myself married!"

"And so you shall," Nelson answered, a grin on his face. "I've arranged a little auction, ladies. You see, our town is in dire need of some female companionship and this was the best way to get women here. You all will be officially married today by our fair pastor and off to your new homes before the sun sets."

An auction? Alysse's smile faded as his words sunk in, feeling like a fool. She was above all these women, with more refinement than the entire room combined! She was not to be treated like this!

"I promise you, ladies," Nelson continued as the doors opened up and maids came through, their trays loaded down with glasses of lemonade. "You will all walk out of here with a husband today. Please, take this time to get ready for I have a group of fine men waiting to make your acquaintance."

Alysse ignored the lemonade. "Nelson please, a moment," she tried as he started to leave. Surely this was some sort of jest. She was meant to marry him, not some common farmer!

He didn't turn, exiting the room before she could reach out for his arm. "Face it," one of the women near her muttered. "We have been duped."

Alysse looked back at the room and straightened her spine. Well, she was a Rearden, which was something these women were not. She would get this straight.

CHAPTER 4

This was not happening, not in his hotel. Robert watched the proceedings as the men clamored to get a better look at the woman on the stage, her eyes wide with fear. When James had stated that this was a party, he had been skeptical, but the money had talked louder than his concerns for what he might be doing.

But he had not expected this.

"She's quite a filly!" a man he hadn't noticed before said, standing behind a crudely built auction podium. "Twenty dollars!"

"Twenty!" someone called out, causing irritation amongst the group. The entire hotel smelled like a barn, the floors he had carefully swept now covered in muck and dust from the street, the door constantly being opened as more men poured through.

What had he done?

"Sold!" the man shouted, pointing to cowboy who had bid twenty dollars. "Enjoy your new wife!"

This had to stop. It was clear these women were not doing this under their own power and he would not have this sort of, of business going on in his hotel! Robert pushed his way through the crowd until he got to the front of the crowd as another woman was led out, her expression one of dismay and anger. "Get your filthy hands off me!"

she shouted to James, who was escorting her to the middle of the room. "You are all a horrid lot!"

He could tell by her accent that she was not from here, her fine clothing giving him another indication that perhaps she had been caught up in something she did not anticipate. She was petite, with a heavy head full of inky black hair tucked in an elegant fashion he had seen in California.

But not here. No, this woman was outside her element.

She turned to face the crowd and he caught a hint of her ice blue eyes as she placed her hands on her hips. There was no hint of fear in her expression. "You! You all should be ashamed! We were duped into this, this fiasco!"

There was the proof he needed. "Stop this!" he shouted, walking to the front of the stage. "This is not right!"

"Give him the loud mouth!" one of the cowboys said from behind Robert. "He's ruining the fun."

James looked at Robert. "These women are all willing participants and it's for the good of the town. Surely you can see that."

"They don't look like willing participants," Robert countered.

"We aren't!" the woman on the stage added. "We all thought we were coming to get married."

"And you are my darling," James replied giving her a smile. "Just, somewhat unconventionally." He then turned back to the crowd. "Who wants this one at ten dollars?"

Robert moved even closer. "This is my hotel and I demand you stop this instance."

James leaned down, a glimmer of greed in his eye. "Are you gonna give me back my money then?"

Robert swallowed. He knew he couldn't. He had put most of the money to use already, lining up some desperate repairs that were needed. There was only a fourth of the money left now. "I thought so," James said, grinning, seeing Robert's look. "My suggestion to you sir, is to bid on a wife for yourself."

"This is despicable," the woman continued to shout as the crowd hooted and hollered at her. "There is no class in this town!"

"But there's plenty of single men wanting a woman," James announced to the crowd. "Ten dollars and she is all yours!"

"Give me twenty and I will take her off your hands," one of the cowboys in the front snickered. Robert looked at the woman in time to catch the dull flush of her cheeks over the embarrassment she was experiencing at the hands of this rowdy crowd.

He could not allow this to continue.

Stepping onto the stage, he shielded the woman from the crowd. "I demand you all leave my hotel now. These women are not for sale!"

James's murderous gaze fell upon him, a sneer on his jovial face. "Fine. You don't want it to happen? Sold to the hotel owner for his meddling! Sir, please escort your 'wife' off the stage so we can continue."

Robert froze at his words. "I-I didn't bid."

"But you did interfere," the auctioneer said.

"I do not want to be married to this man!" the woman cried as they were both pushed off the stage. Robert was dumbfounded. What had he done? He didn't need a wife! He needed to save his hotel!

"This cannot be happening," the woman muttered next to him, the scent of lavender emanating from her. "I am in a horrid nightmare."

"If you are, then I am as well," he muttered, running a hand through his hair as the next woman was paraded on the stage, looking a bit more like she enjoyed it than the first two. What had started as a positive mark for his hotel had gone downhill rapidly and he couldn't do a thing about it.

Not one thing.

CHAPTER 5

*A*lysse wanted to shout madly to the crowd, letting out all her frustrations on the blood thirsty cowboys that were leering at them like they were some sort of cattle for their amusement. How had she gotten into this mess?

There had been a moment when the gentleman standing next to her had been a savior, attempting to stop this farce of an auction. She had thought he would accomplish his task, until she overheard the remark about the funds he had been provided to host this sort of function.

He was no savior, he was in on this-this abomination-as well!

And now she was about to be married to him.

Her heart full of anger and despair, she watched as Desiree flaunted herself on stage, clearly enjoying the attention given by the crowd. She wished to be back in Savannah, before her father had lost everything and she was someone important to society-to Stephen. Her mother would be alive and doting on her only daughter as she had done all of Alysse's life.

Oh, what she wouldn't give to have her mother's guidance at this very moment!

Alysse straightened her shoulders as she stole a glance at the man beside her, who was watching the proceedings in horror. He was tall, with fair hair and vivid blue eyes. She could see his shoulders were quite broad under his shirt and a peculiar warmth spread in her belly as she thought about how he had attempted to stop the auction. Perhaps she had been too hard on him in her mind. Surely, he needed the funds for something and the gentleman running the auction had taken advantage of this.

He turned, and she found herself staring into his eyes. "I-I apologize for this," he stammered, running a hand through his shock of blond hair.

Alysse fought the urge to smooth it down for him, her hands itching to do just that. "It's not your fault."

He blew out a breath. "I have a bit of money. I can secure your passage back to wherever you came from."

The kind gesture touched her heart. She was no more than a stranger to him, but he was willing to provide for her? "I... that is very kind of you."

"Whoa now, wait a second!"

They both turned to see a man holding what appeared to be a bible in his hand, a grin on his face. "No one is leaving this hotel without the sacrament of marriage performed. I will not have these couples that God brought together living in a sinful nature!"

"I-we are not getting married," the man next to her said, his voice rough. "I cannot believe you are allowing this to happen, preacher."

The preacher had the grace to look embarrassed, his grin sliding off his face. "I'm only doing what is right and the right thing is to make sure these women are protected by the men that win them. Surely you can't find fault in that Robert."

Robert. That was his name. "I will not wed a stranger," Robert said in a low voice.

"Neither will I," Alysse added, causing both men to look at her. "I will not go into this marriage willingly."

The preacher looked at them both before shrugging his shoulders. "Well then, you shall be bathed in the devil's sin until you do. When you are ready, come to the church and I will bind this marriage according to God's Holy Will."

"Wait a minute," Robert began, but the preacher was already walking away, whistling as he disappeared into the crowd. Alysse watched him leave, wondering what fine people in Savannah would think of this turn of events. She was about to live in sin with a man she did not know.

"I apologize for this."

Alysse turned to her 'husband', seeing the regret in his eyes. She could take up his offer to get on the coach and never look back, but where would that take her? She had no money of her own, no family to run to. She could not go back home. She could not go back to the life she was leading just a year ago, before her life was turned upside down.

She had nothing.

A sob escaped her, and he paled. "I have money."

"I have nowhere to go," she said pitifully, not liking the sound of her own voice. "It would do me no good."

Robert looked at her before sighing. "I can offer you a room upstairs, free of charge, until you decide. It is not much, but it will be a dry, warm place for you to lay your head."

The crowd grew louder and she found Robert touching her elbow, gesturing for her to follow him. Her heart heavy, as she did so, not seeing another choice. She had nowhere to go to and he was being more than sympathetic to her needs.

He might be the only friend she had right now.

They walked up a set of dark stairs to the second level of the building, the sounds of what was happening below starting to muffle in the distance. "I never thought," he said to himself as they passed rows of doors. "That was not what he told me he was going to do today."

"Seems we have all been duped," she added, softly, as he paused in front of a door. Robert looked back at her and Alysse felt her breath still in her chest. He was quite handsome, far more than Stephen had been. "You're right, we have."

She colored as he opened the door and she stepped into the room, the smell of dust tickling her nose. "I haven't had a chance to clean these rooms," he said, softly. "But they are furthest away from the other guests. You should be comfortable here."

Alysse looked around the small room and fought the urge to cry. This was her life now and she best get used to the fact that she was no longer the person she longed to be.

CHAPTER 6

*S*he was lovely...

Robert waited anxiously as she looked about the room, seeing the distaste on her face. It was the best he could offer at the moment and still, looking at her clothing, it didn't seem enough.

She turned toward him and extended her hand, her bottom lip trembling. "Alysse Rearden."

He took her hand in his, feeling the delicate bones encased in the white glove. "Robert Chastain."

She nodded, and he dropped her hand, feeling a steady stream of electricity travel up his arm. Up close he could see the flecks of dark blue in her eyes, the fine features of her face. If she hadn't reacted the way she had, he imagined she would have been fought over by the crowd downstairs.

How did someone so delicate, so refined, get in this mess? He longed to ask her, but figured it was none of his business, she'd tell him if she wanted.

"Well, I am sure you have many questions," she said, her smile trembling on her lips. "And I will provide the answers as I see fit."

"You do not owe me any explanations," he stated, holding up his hand. "Take the room. We can work out something until you are back on your feet."

Her eyes widened slightly, and she immediately looked flustered. Robert rubbed the back of his neck with his hand, feeling awkward at talking with her. He had met many a fine lady in California, but never one to carry on a conversation with. This one was down on her luck, he could tell and after today, well, he just wanted to make it all go away.

"Thank you," she finally said, her voice soft. "I can earn my keep."

He walked toward the door. "We can discuss that in the morning. Get some rest. I usually fix breakfast just after seven for myself."

"See you then," she said as he exited the room. Once in the hall, Robert let out a long slow breath, forcing his feet to walk toward the stairs. First the auction, now this. Why had he been so greedy and accepted the money?

If he hadn't, his life would be the same as it always was.

Fortunately, the crowd was starting to disperse as he made his way back down the stairs. Robert marched over to James and wanted nothing more than to plant his fist in the man's ruddy face. "Pack your things and go."

James looked up, a handful of bills in his hand. "I plan to. This was a complete success I might add! Your town will be thanking me that I was able to bring some women to their lives."

Robert advanced on him, his fists at his side. "What you brought were scared women who thought they were marrying a certain kind of man."

"What I brought," James said, as he placed the money in the inside pocket of his coat, "Is women who were going to marry a stranger regardless. So what if their husband is not whom they thought he would be? At least they have one." He then reached into his valise and pulled out a worn envelope, handing it to Robert. "Here. This was your wife's letter. I figured you would like to get to know her."

Robert snatched the letter. "She is not my wife."

James shrugged. "It's not my matter any longer. Good day sir and thank you for your assistance."

Robert watched, dumbfounded, as James walked out of the hotel lobby, whistling as he did so. No one other than the people in this town would believe what had transpired here today.

Shaking his head, Robert walked back to the counter, easing behind the solid wood surface as he looked at the letter in his hand. It wouldn't be right to read it, would it? But if his hotel guest was to stay for an undetermined amount of time, he should at least see if she had someone looking for her.

He slid his finger under the flap and extracted a piece of cream colored stationary, the faint smell of rosewater wafting from it. It was thick and finely made and as Robert opened the letter, he could see the stamp of an A on the top, intertwined with flowers.

Something this extravagant was quite expensive. What was Alysse's story?

Looking at her elegant scrawl, he began to read.

My Dear Sir, it began. *I have read your plight and wish to accept your advertisement for a wife. I come from a prominent family and have all the fine skills that a lady should have. I can plan and host a formal party, play the harpsichord, direct servants in their daily tasks, and have learned the fine art of entertaining. My education is from the finest finishing schools in all of Georgia and if you choose me to be your wife, I promise that you will not regret your choice.*

It was signed with her name, Alysse Elizabeth Rearden. Robert re-read the letter before choking on his laughter and dismay. The woman above the stairs was not a woman used to hard labor nor did she possess any of the skills that he desperately needed. She could not cook and while hosting lavish parties could be a benefit to the hotel, he had to garner customers in order to do that.

Robert lay the letter on the counter and rubbed his hand over his face, feeling hopeless. He needed some help in the hotel, though he could not afford to pay anyone. He needed customers, patrons that would pay with more than just a few coins. He needed something to drive them in droves to his family's legacy, something that his ancestors would be proud of.

Most of all, he needed to not fail. To fail and potentially lose the hotel would be devastation to him. This hotel was his family, it was what they had fought so hard to achieve and Robert would not let them down.

CHAPTER 7

*A*lysse woke up the next morning with a renewed focus on her life. She dressed carefully, frowning at the number of wrinkles that were now pressed into the fabric of her gown. There was little she could do, other than stand outside in the Texas heat and allow the wrinkles to fall out of the silk fabric. There was no maid to attend to her, something she had grown accustom to not having over the last few months anyway. The family friend that she and her mother had stayed with had not provided a lady's maid, and Alysse had painstakingly learned how to keep up appearances when one had to keep them up herself.

Sliding her feet into her sturdy boots, she took one last look in the mirror that hung above the dresser. The girl staring back was not one she recognized, even after all this time. She looked older, her eyes not holding the allure of who she was any longer. There was a sharpness to them, one that she knew came with the burden of procuring her own way in life now.

There was no one to depend on, no one that was going to get her out of this except herself.

She straightened her shoulders and walked out of the room, the

smell of eggs and bacon filling the air. Her stomach rumbled apprecia-
tively as she made her way down the stairs, locating the kitchen by the
smell of the food. It had been quite some time since she had a decent
meal, surviving on tea and small sandwiches on the train to conserve
her small ration of funds.

How on earth was she going to afford this hotel? This food? Alysse
was not one for charity nor did she even wish to marry the hotel
owner just to have a roof over her head.

She would have to think of a way to repay his kindness.

Rounding the corner, she stopped in the doorway, surprised to see
Robert at the large stove, humming to himself as he tended to the pots
and pans on the surface. There was no one else in the room, not even
at the small table tucked in the corner.

Where was his staff?

Clearing her throat, Alysse announced her presence. "Good
morning."

"Good morning," Robert replied, not looking up. "Have a seat at
the table. I am almost done here."

She was not used to having a gentleman not fawn over her dress,
or the style of her hair. Though she was not vain in the slightest, the
burn was still present in her chest as she did as he had instructed,
seating herself at the table. It had been difficult to survive the last year
without her usual society friends around her. Alysse had thought that
perhaps they would have taken pity on her, taken her under
their wing.

But that had not been the case.

Robert joined her at the table, sliding a plate in front of her before
seating himself. Alysse looked at the perfectly cooked eggs and crispy
bacon, her stomach gnawing against her side. She shouldn't eat this
sort of fare. Her mother would scold her for eating such food. A lady
ate very little in the morning.

"Is something wrong?"

Alysse looked up at Robert. "No, not at all. I am not used to this
sort of fare."

He chuckled as he picked up his fork. "Here on the frontier, you never know when you will get to eat again. My mother taught me to eat a hearty breakfast, so it will last you all day."

"Where are your parents?" she asked, as he dug into his eggs.

His fork stilled on the path to his mouth. "They are no longer on this earth."

She drew in a breath. "I apologize for asking." She shouldn't have pried.

He waved a hand at her. "'Tis fine. They have been gone for quite some time, perishing in a carriage accident when I was ten. I was raised by my uncle."

"Mine are gone as well," she said softly. There was no reason to tell him that her father was still alive. To her, he was gone. She would never see him again, never smell his aftershave as he would hug her in the evenings. Never again would she see her mother gaze at him with love in her eyes or laugh when he would bring her the flowers he knew she enjoyed.

Her stomach twisted and Alysse abruptly stood. "I-I'm sorry. I must go."

Without waiting for his response, she hurried out of the room, up to her own room before the tears started to fall. Why had her life been the one to be ruined with so much devastation? Alysse thought back to the moment when her father had been arrested. She and her mother had huddled together in their elegant home, the lunch untouched on the table. For hours they had sat like that, the numbness of what had happened coursing through their bodies. At that moment, Alysse had felt helpless.

Never in her life had she felt so helpless.

So, she had gone to her room and sat on her bed for hours, twisting the elegant ring that Stephen had put on her finger as she attempted to plot how to get her family out of this horrible situation.

There had been no way to do so. No matter what avenue she tried, pleading with her father's former friends or discussing their plight with the finest lawyers in all of Savannah, no one would help them. Her father was guilty, and the mountain of evidence had proven so.

Alysse wiped the tears from her eyes as she crossed the room, looking out of the dirt streaked window at the street below. That had been her past, this had to be her future. She had no other choice, nothing about her former life that was going to rescue her in the end.

Oh, what was she going to do?

CHAPTER 8

*R*obert stood in the doorway of his dining room, his arms crossed over his chest. When he had conjured up the idea, he had thought of the grand hotel dining rooms of California, the ones with the crushed velvet seating and fine oak tables covered in white tablecloths. Once Robert had eaten in such a dining room establishment, the food finer than anything he had ever eaten. It was then he had decided to create the same sort of experience back in Texas.

If only it had come to fruition. There was no part of the dining room before him that resembled the fine establishment, the entire room in sore need of a good dusting. His tables did not have any fresh white linen cloths on them.

Had he dreamed too big?

"Robert?" a voice from behind him queried.

Surprised, Robert turned to see Alysse standing a few feet away, her hands clasped in front of her. He could tell she had been crying and he was at a loss of how to comfort her. "Alysse."

"I wish to apologize for my behavior earlier," she said in a rush. "I am a bit homesick, that is all."

He nodded. "Of course. I understand. Think nothing of it."

WHEN LOVE COMES TO TOWN

She gave him a tentative smile and the blood rushed to his head. She was perhaps the prettiest thing he had ever seen. "What are you doing?"

Clearing his throat, Robert forced himself to think. "I was, well it's silly really."

"Tell me," she replied, tilting her head to the side.

He ran a hand through his hair, suddenly nervous. "I wanted to open a dining room in the hotel."

Her eyes widened, and she walked to the room, peering in. "It seems you have everything in order."

"Except the patrons," he said with a chuckle.

"Who does the cooking?"

Robert felt his cheeks flush. "I would have to, until I could afford to hire someone."

Alysse moved further into the space, drawing back the dusting cloths that covered the table. "Can you make a good pot of tea?"

Robert was confused. "Tea?"

She turned to him, clasping her hands behind her back. There was a broad smile on her face. "I have an idea."

"By all means," Robert said, feeling a spark of excitement deep within him.

She moved about the room, her hands touching each piece of furniture that was in the room lightly, the dust billowing as her skirts moved about the floor. "Why don't we host a tea party, for the women of course? Now that the town has more women, it's going to be the women that bring you customers."

A tea party. That was far from the dining room he had envisioned. That and he didn't see how it would draw customers.

The look on his face must have shown his confusion as she laughed, her eyes sparkling. "The tea party would only be the beginning. We could advertise a special night, a re-opening of the hotel and its new dining room! It is the perfect way to garner business."

Robert thought about her plan. There was only one problem that he could think of. "People in these parts won't spend a nickel on a meal that they could cook themselves."

Alysse thought for a moment before her eyes lit up. "What if we did it for free? Do you think they would come then?"

A free meal? Robert was barely making ends meet with the money that he had earned from the auction. "I cannot afford that."

"What if they were small meals, like a tasting?" Alysse suggested. "Enough to have people spread the word."

Robert stared at the woman that had burst into his life when he had least anticipated it. Was this why she was here? "You're wonderful!"

She gave him a shy smile, looking away. "I-I want to help. I'm not good at many things, but throwing a party, that I am very good at it."

Grinning, he joined her at the table, pulling the sheet away from the wood. "Seems then, that we will need to get to work." This was going to work. This was a perfect way to showcase the food he could provide while getting his future customers to come into the hotel for more than just a woman auction.

And if he could get the women on his side, they would influence their husbands to come back for more. He might have to keep his price low, but word would spread like wildfire and before he would know it, the town would be sending their visitors to his hotel for more than just lodging for the night. Looking at Alysse, he caught her eye. "I would like to partner with you. I-can't pay you now, but perhaps if this is successful, then there could be a position for you."

She drew in a breath. "I will work for the roof over my head if you will allow me to do so. I-I don't know much about running a hotel, but I am willing to learn."

"What about your reputation?" he asked, knowing he had to remind her of such. Living in a hotel with an unmarried man would bound to bring rumors and he didn't want to harm her reputation.

She gave a little laugh, running her hand over the surface of the table. "My reputation is far gone. As long as you can live with the fact that you have an outspoken southern belle under your roof, I can live with the fact that I am living in sin, as the preacher pointed out."

Robert chuckled, reaching across the table with his hand outstretched. "I believe we have a deal then."

28

She laid her hand in his and he felt the warmth of her skin seeping through his, sending goosebumps up his arm. "A partnership then."

Robert was quick to end their handshake, a thousand things running through his mind. This had to work.

He had no other ideas or options.

CHAPTER 9

*A*lysse threw herself into her work, now feeling as if she might have a purpose in life with this dining room and this hotel. It was clear to her that Robert needed help and after finding out that he had larger aspirations than just the hotel, she felt the need to help him. Never mind that she was living under his roof, as an unmarried woman. Her mother would have a fit if she knew what her daughter was doing.

Yet her mother was no longer here to scold her. No one was here to help her through life and Alysse knew she had to figure it out for herself.

Humming a tune, she wiped down the last of the tables, the smell of beeswax polish clinging to the air. The room itself was quite large and Robert had purchased various sizes of tables to accommodate the large space. Already she could picture each table graced with a white linen tablecloth, a single flower in its vase in the middle of the table.

Now, if only she could locate those items.

Alysse walked through the dining room to the lobby of the hotel, the sun shining through the double panes of stained glass that graced the two front doors. Robert was not at his desk as she imagined him to be.

Turning down the hall, she passed the kitchen, seeing no sign of him as well. In their planning, he stated that he would draw up a menu for her approval for the tea party and she was surprised at how giddy he had sounded about her idea. Someone was not looking at her past, her family name or the amount of funds they'd had. Someone was seeing her as a person and her insides warmed at the thought. Robert seemed to be a nice man, a kind one, though he would have had to be to allow her to stay here without paying.

She hoped that was not the reason he had no funds.

With a sigh, Alysse continued down the hall, until she located the room she had been looking for. It was the storage room and her eyes rounded as she saw the mountains of dishes that were stacked neatly on the shelves, the delicate china in every color and pattern. There was also a pile of neatly folded tablecloths, wrapped carefully in paper to keep from the dusting tinting their color. Stepping farther into the room, she found other decorations that could be used in the tea party, including several teapots to match the china. A thought occurred to her, making her grin in a very unladylike manner. They could have a different set for each table.

"What are you doing in here?"

Alysse jumped and turned to find Robert staring at her, his arms crossed over his chest. "I was looking for the china closet."

"You found it," he chuckled, sweeping his hand at the supplies that lined the walls. "This is my family's legacy as well. My mother used to joke that she could serve the entire state of Texas on her dishes and still never run out."

It was clear to Alysse that he enjoyed talking about his family. How long had he been on his own? It must have been lonely here in this hotel, without people to love. "I promise I will not use them all."

"Good," he said with a wink. "Because we are the dish washers as well. Please remember that."

Alysse looked down at her hands, the hands she had been so careful of all her life. Wash dishes? She hadn't washed anything before.

31

"I'll teach you what you wish to know," Robert said softly, his voice low.

She looked up at him, that peculiar warmth sliding through her veins. She wanted to ask him to talk like that again, just so she could feel the shudder of her spine, a pleasant shudder mind you. "I-I'm afraid I will have to learn."

"Everyone has to learn at some point in their life," Robert replied, clearing his throat. "Do you know what you wish to use out of here?"

Alysse shook her head. She would need to spend some time deciding. "Not right yet." Walking toward him, her foot caught the edge of a crate and she let out a cry as she pitched forward, her hands blindly finding something to grasp to keep herself from hitting the ground.

In an instant, she was curled against a warm, solid chest, the smell of Robert's aftershave overpowering her senses. "Easy now," he said into her ear, his hands tightening around her. "There's many breakable things in this room."

"Good thing I didn't reach for the shelf then," she teased, shakily, her heart racing in her chest as she felt his warmth around her. Oh my. This was far different than the chaste touches that she and Stephen had ever shared together.

Alysse had never felt so-so alive before.

"Tis a good thing," he murmured before placing her back on her feet. "Are you all right?"

"I'm fine," she said, her voice somewhat shaky. Suddenly she felt shy in his presence, new feelings surrounding them that were not there before. "Thank you."

"You're welcome," he said, seemingly undisturbed by their encounter. Perhaps she had imagined it all. Perhaps her heart wanted to cling to the closest person that showed any compassion to her.

Perhaps this was all a dream.

Alysse cleared her throat and took a few steps back from Robert, flustered at what she was feeling for the man she barely knew. "I assume we need to pick out the patterns then for the tea party?"

He nodded, clasping his hands behind his back. "You pick them out, I will carry them to the kitchen."

Alysse gave him a quick nod as she turned toward the shelves, grateful to have her back to the hotel owner. What was happening to her?

What was happening to her life?

CHAPTER 10

*R*obert allowed a long pull on his cheroot, leaning against the post outside of the hotel. The town itself was quiet, though there were lamps lit in the building across the street. Someone had purchased the old saloon apparently. While he was glad to see the town reviving itself, the last thing he wanted to see again was the saloon. The previous owner was a hard man and many a fight had spilled out into the street on any given night.

It didn't bode well for business.

Sighing, he forced himself to look at the night sky, the stars unable to be visible tonight. For the first time in a few weeks, there was a threat of rain in the air and for that, he was grateful. Perhaps it would be a welcome change to the unbearable heat they had suffered through.

But the rain and the saloon were not the only things on his mind.

Robert took another draw on the cheroot as he thought about Alysse. Today, in the china closet, he had held her in his arms, not wishing to let go. She had been so soft and pliant and for a split second, he had thought about kissing her. They barely knew each other yet he felt this connection to his Southern belle. Had she felt the same? Robert wasn't sure, but he hoped so.

It was more than just needing her help with the dining room. He wanted to get to know her as a person and if his feelings were any indication, he wanted to know her as a woman he could care for.

The door opened behind him and Robert stilled, the sweet smell of rosewater mingling with the earthy scent of his cheroot. They had shared a simple meal tonight, talking over their dinner about the menu he would prepare for both events. The sparkle in her eyes had stayed with him long after he had left her in the dining room, setting out the plates.

"I believe the room is ready," she said, after a moment, her arms wrapping around the post on the other side of the stairs. "I will go around tomorrow to garner us some business."

"The stage will also come through tomorrow," Robert added, grounding out his cheroot on the bottom of his boot.

"Do you usually get any patrons?" Alysse asked.

"A few," he relied and shrugged, turning to face her. "Though I believe the last one brought a permanent member of the hotel."

She flashed him a smile. "Permanent? I'm not too sure about that."

Her words echoed through his brain. He wouldn't mind if she was a permanent resident. He was enjoying having someone around. "What would you do if you were not here, Alysse?"

She gave a soft laugh, something desolate in the sound. "I'm not sure. There was a time in my life I had my future already planned for me, but now, everything has changed."

He wanted to ask, to find out more about her, but the way she said the words, it was clearly painful for her. "I can understand. My life is not what I had anticipated it to be."

"No?"

Robert shook his head. "I imagined I would come back here and pick up where I had left off, with a hotel full of people and my uncle standing behind the desk, his smile greeting them as they walked through the lobby." He sighed. "But I never imagined my uncle would pass on before I could get home."

"I'm sorry," Alysse said softly, leaning her head against the post. "I-I know what it feels like to lose someone close to you."

He imagined she did. Any woman that was willing to give up her reputation for a roof over their head either had nowhere to stay or no one to go home to. For Alysse, Robert could only consider both. "Are you nervous about tomorrow?" he asked, changing from the painful subject.

The light in her eyes returned and she gave him a smile that had his heart racing. "I-yes I am a bit nervous, but I believe that I can get the women to the party. The rest, well, we will just have to see about that."

"You will be a success," he promised her. "They will all want to be your friend."

"I hope so," she admitted, pushing away from the post. For a moment, Robert thought about sliding his arm around her waist again, pulling her against him. That was what the entire town was likely thinking about the both of them anyway.

But he wanted her to feel the same. He wanted her to come to him willingly and without worry that she would lose the roof over her head. Now was not the time. "Good night Alysse."

She paused at the door, her hand on the knob. "Good night Robert."

He waited until she had made her way inside before he let out a breath, turning his attention back to the cloudy night sky once more.

~

The next morning, Robert stood on the sidewalk, a cup of steaming coffee in his hand as he watched Alysse head across the street on her mission. She was dressed in another one of her fine gowns, though he had seen the wariness in her eyes over breakfast. She was concerned this was not going to work.

Robert, on the other hand, knew she would be successful. Her charming smile, the way she drew him in with her eyes, people were not going to be able to turn her down. He imagined she could charm anybody in doing what she wanted, him included.

The sound of the stagecoach caught his attention and Robert

watched as it crested the hill in the distance, finishing his cup before throwing out the remnants on the dusty street. A stagecoach would bring customers and he had much to do to be ready for them. Robert cast one last look at the departing Alysse before walking inside, sending up a prayer to whomever was listening above for the woman who was rapidly stealing his heart.

CHAPTER 11

$\mathcal{A}$lysse walked into the mercantile with her head held high, not showing an ounce of fear even though it roiled in her stomach something horrid. She knew that the mercantile was nothing more than a place for town gossip and if she wished to spread the word about the tea party to the women, she would need to make some sort of connection with the owner.

A young woman was standing behind the counter as she approached, her eyes traveling over the last remaining gown Alysse had left to wear. "May I help you?"

Alysse gave her a wide smile, remembering what her father had taught her. If she could win them over with a smile and a kind word, then the rest would fall into place. "I am Alysse."

"Claudette," the young woman said slowly. "What may I help you with, Alysse?"

Alysse sat her reticule on the counter. "I am hosting a tea party at the hotel in two days and need your assistance in spreading the word to the rest of the women in town."

Claudette chuckled. "You want me to tell everyone else?"

She nodded. "I imagine you can do that rather well."

Claudette stared at her. "What might be in it for me?"

Alysse had been anticipating this. With a wide smile, she leaned forward. "If this party is successful, I will be holding another to open our dining room. Would you like to come work at the hotel?"

Claudette's eyes widened, and she looked around, as if someone was going to listen in at any moment. "I-is Robert still there?"

Alysse tamped down a spurt of jealousy that flared in her chest. Why was the young woman asking about Robert?

"I-I mean I was just curious," Claudette quickly said, a flush coming across her cheeks. "With you staying there and all."

"Of course, he's still there," Alysse replied sharper than she had intended. She did not like the idea of Robert and Claudette. Robert was hers and hers only.

But as soon as the thought hit her, Alysse was forced to push it aside. Robert was his own man and if he had already promised something to the young woman in front of her, she wasn't going to stand in his way. They were not wed, nor did she imagine he had any feelings for her other than a mutual partnership. "I am just helping him with the dining room he will be opening up soon. That's all."

Claudette didn't look like she believed her. "So, you are a guest at the hotel? Everyone's been talking about you women who came in, thinking you were getting hitched to the same man. I just thought, well, that Robert had purchased you."

Alysse allowed herself to laugh as if it was the silliest thing she had ever heard, though deep down, she had wished now that she hadn't put up such a fight when they had the chance to become man and wife. "I am a guest but want to help out Robert and the hotel. We have formed a partnership of sorts to make the hotel a success."

"Oh," Claudette replied, her cheeks coloring. "Well, he is a wonderful man. I will spread the word about your party if it's gonna help him."

Alysse bit her lip to keep from telling the woman not to do such a thing, the jealousy both surprising and overwhelming at the same time. She needed this to happen. Robert needed this to happen. She would have to put her personal feelings aside. "Thank you." Quickly she gave the woman the information about both the tea party and the upcoming dancing and dinner they had already planned and walked out of the store into the stifling heat, seeing that the stagecoach had already arrived. Robert would be happy if they got one or two customers to stay the night and she would help him ensure their comfort. A few days in his hotel and she was scrubbing dishes with her hands, sweeping the floor and learning how to use the wash tub to not only wash her clothing but that of the hotel as well. He had turned her into a maid, but she didn't mind.

Alysse crossed the street, a wry smile coming to her face. A maid. Never in her life had she imagined she would be a maid of anything, having been pampered all her life. While she should be protesting the labor, refusing to do the menial tasks that had been so beneath her a year ago, Alysse found herself waking up this morning looking forward to the day and what it held. It gave her that sense of purpose she had been missing, that belonging that being here at the hotel had provided, even if it had only been a few days.

"Miss!"

Alysse turned to see a man approaching her, a kind smile on his face. It was the preacher from the auction, the one who had scolded them for not marrying. "Pastor."

"You remembered," he said and grinned as he reached her side. "How are you faring?"

"Just fine," she answered as she shielded her eyes with her hand. "My host has been more than generous."

The pastor stepped forward, searching her face for signs of duress. "Robert is a wonderful friend. I would have imagined nothing less from him. You are fortunate to have ended up with him, but I hoped that you would seek out my assistance if this situation is not what you wished it to be."

Alysse smiled up at his friendly expression. "I know you think less of me for staying."

His smile was wide as he shook his head, tipping his hat toward her. "No ma'am. I believe you are a better woman than I originally thought. Take care of my friend."

Alysse watched him go, her feelings for Robert gnawing at her heart. Oh, how she wanted to!

CHAPTER 12

*R*obert watched nervously from the wings of the dining room as the women started to enjoy their sandwiches, surprised at how many women had shown up at the hotel today. It seemed that Claudette had done a fine job spreading the word about the free tea time and every woman in and around the town had descended upon his dining room, eager to enjoy their morning.

There were all sorts of women, young and old seated at the tables that Alysse had so lovingly designed, each table having their own set of china and bunch of wildflowers that he and Alysse had picked just yesterday. While he had no vases, they had found some canning jars in the pantry and to him, they were looking more at home than anything else.

Especially amongst their company.

Shifting his feet, he watched as Alysse moved from table to table, chatting with the women and winning them over with her smile. His heart was bursting with pride at what she had been able to accomplish in such a short time here, excited at what they could continue to accomplish together after today.

Alysse looked up and he grinned at her, seeing her eyes sparkle as she returned his smile before turning her attention back to the women. She was a surprise to him, someone he had not even considered to be what he needed. They got along quite well and his feelings about her, well, they had only grown over the last few days.

Would she be amenable to becoming his wife?

Robert cleared his throat, surprised at his line of thought. A wife? He hadn't thought about having a wife until she had blown into his life. But now, he knew he didn't want to let her go.

It was far more than just what she was trying to do for his hotel.

It was what she was doing to his life that was causing him to think about this decision.

The bell above the door tinkled and he was forced to table his thoughts for now, walking to the lobby with a smile on his face. The lobby was full of weary travelers, all looking around with some wariness. "Can I help you?"

"Thank goodness," the woman exclaimed, gripping the arm of the man next to her. They were both well dressed, and Robert felt the stirring of excitement in his veins. "We were afraid that this, this hotel was not in service."

"It is," Robert said as he pulled out his registration log. "How may I help you?"

The man stepped forward, his wife clinging to his arm. "I'm afraid we are on our honeymoon and the coach has broken an axle. It's likely we will be here for a few days."

"I have plenty of room," Robert said, nodding to the others that were behind the couple. "For all of you."

"I can pay," the man said, pulling out a clip and peeling off a few bills before pushing them in Robert's direction. "I imagine that will be enough to get your finest room?"

Robert stared at the money. It was far more than he was going to ask for and as for the room, well, they were all the same. "Of course. Meals are provided."

"We will take one as well," the other couple responded, placing money on the counter.

Robert gathered up the bills and slid them into his pocket. Alysse was going to be so excited to hear that they had more guests to entertain. He would seat them in the dining room tonight, test out some of the recipes that they were going to serve at the party in a few days time.

"If you will just sign here," he forced out, hiding his excitement. "I will get your keys."

The men did as he requested, and he handed them their keys, the women bestowing grateful smiles on Robert as he showed them to their rooms. The man turned toward him and stuck out his hand. "Thank you."

Robert shook his hand. "I'm Robert if you need anything."

"Stephen," the man replied with an easy smile. "Stephen Filmort."

Robert nodded and moved to the next man, who gave him a nod as he took his key. Both couples seemed to be well to do, though Robert wasn't so sure about the first one as they made their way to their rooms. There was something that made him pause, though he couldn't put his finger on it.

~

*A*fter the women left the dining room, Robert went in to clean up the dishes with a giddy Alysse. "It worked!" she replied happily as she stacked the plates. "They all promised they would bring their husbands to the party and spread the word to their neighbors. This was exactly what we were hoping for."

"Thanks to you," Robert reminded her as he carried the plates to the kitchen. She followed close behind, her arms ladened with dishes and they set them gently on the counter near the sink. "I had a few travelers check in while you were entertaining."

"Oh, that's wonderful Robert!" she exclaimed, turning to face him.

Robert looked at Alysse and without thinking leaned over to press his lips on hers, elated that she was so happy for them both. He could hear her gasp before he pulled back, the sweetness of her own lips on his making him ache for more. "I-I apologize."

She shook her head, a dull blush on her cheeks as she touched her fingers to her mouth. "Don't be. That was nice."

WHEN LOVE COMES TO TOWN

Nice wasn't the word he would normally be excited about, but she wasn't upset that he had kissed her. "After this party," he started. "I would like for us to discuss the future, Alysse."

Her lips parted, and Robert fought the urge to kiss her again. "I would like that Robert."

Robert grinned then, unable to help it. Everything was falling so nicely into place that he was afraid to even breathe just in case this was a dream. He had his hotel, a budding dining room, travelers in his rooms, and Alysse. Oh, he had Alysse and he had no intentions of letting her go.

CHAPTER 13

*A*lysse hummed to herself as she fashioned her hair into a cascade of curls, wondering if she was overdoing it for supper tonight. With the travelers in the hotel, she wanted to show them that even a dusty town such as this could be civilized and have them spread the word to their friends far and wide.

So, she had dressed in her finest gown and styled her hair to rival any hairstyle her former maid had done. The sparkle in her eyes and flush on her cheeks was not something she had caused.

No, they were there because she was happy.

Standing, Alysse brushed the wrinkles out of her gown and drew in a breath, thinking about the kiss she and Robert had shared mere hours ago. It had been wonderful, and she had found herself wishing he would kiss her again. She felt comfortable with him, safe with him and could not wait until they could speak of their future together. If he proposed marriage, she would accept. Even after nearly a week here, she knew this was where she was supposed to be. Her life, the struggles, they had all led to Robert and her life would not be complete if she left this hotel, left him.

Looking in the mirror once more, she walked out of her room and down the stairs, her slippers barely making a sound on the wooden floor. Tonight, she would play the role of consummate hostess, Robert's right hand to make this dinner a success. If they could win over this group of travelers, then there would be no limits to what else they could achieve.

The smell of roasting meat wafted through the air as she approached the kitchen, seeing Robert hard at work at preparing the evening meal. For a moment, she watched him, seeing the flawless dance he did from the stove to the plates, carefully spooning the gravy from the roast onto the potatoes she had helped peel earlier.

Though her hands ached from the task, her heart had never felt more alive.

He turned, and she gave him a wide smile. "Everything smells lovely."

He chuckled as he returned the spoon to its holder. "I hope it tastes just as good."

"I'm sure it will," she said, walking over to take a few of the plates herself. They had already discussed perhaps hiring a local towns person to help if this was successful, though Alysse was rapidly learning how to monitor their spending so that they didn't get too ahead of themselves. "Shall we sweep them off their feet?"

He gave her a wink as he gathered the rest of the plates. "After you."

Alysse felt her heart warm with his fond gaze, knowing in her heart of hearts this was where she wanted to remain. Perhaps after this night, she would tell him that. Would he want to make it official? Of course, the affection was there. They were a good team.

"What?" Robert asked.

Alysse flushed as she realized she was staring. "I was-I think we make a good team."

"I believe we do," Robert said in that low voice she dearly loved to hear. "And after tonight, perhaps we can plan our future."

Before he had stated after the party but now, she didn't want to wait any longer.

Giving him a nod, Alysse marched out of the kitchen, her head held high as she walked to the dining room. There were two couples in the dining room, seated at separate tables. Alysse walked to the first table and set the full plates down carefully so as not to spill the food. "I hope this food is to your liking."

"Alysse?"

A familiar voice sent chills down her spine as she straightened, staring into the face of her former fiancé. "S-Stephen?"

His eyes swept over her in surprise. "Whatever are you doing here?"

She was at a loss for words. Looking over, he recognized the woman he had become engaged to right before Alysse had left Savannah. "Sarah. You are looking lovely."

The woman, who had been one of her dearest friends, had the grace to flush, the gold band on her hand catching Alysse's eye. Then she realized why they were here. Moving her gaze back to Stephen, she stared him in the face. "You got married."

His face turned red. "What did you think was going to happen Alysse? I couldn't-it was necessary. Are you working in this hotel?"

The way he said the words, with the same haughtiness she would have used in the past, made her ill. Not because she was indeed working at this hotel, but more so because she had been a horrid person when she had been in Savannah. What she was doing, what Robert was attempting to do, it was good solid work for their future. Clearing her throat, she stared him down. "Why yes, I am working here. Not everyone can have their way paved for them."

"You did at one time," Sarah said with a giggle. "Too bad your father was found to be a criminal, Alysse."

Her words were loud enough for the entire dining room to hear and Alysse knew that Robert had heard who she truly was. Her face lost all color, but she managed to give the woman she had considered a friend a tight nod. "You're right, I did, and I can only be grateful that I am no longer like you."

Sarah gasped, and Stephen stood, but she didn't give them any more of her time, hurrying out of the dining room before she dissolved into tears. Robert was likely going to ask her to leave his hotel and she deserved for him to do just that. He didn't need someone like her, someone with a past sullying the good work he was attempting to do here. She didn't want to cause him trouble nor did she wish to cause him any heartache in the long run.

Even if her own heart was breaking in the process.

CHAPTER 14

*R*obert watched as Alysse hurried out of the dining room, not fast enough to see the look on her face as she did so. He had heard the remarks, heard the accusations and couldn't be prouder of the way Alysse had handled the situation. He didn't care about her past, only that she was willing to stay here for her future.

With him.

"Excuse me," he said to the couple before walking over to the table that Alysse had just fled from. The man gave him a smirk as he approached, and Robert fought the urge to plant his fist in his face. "Get out."

The man's smirk faded. "What?"

Robert braced his hands on the table, leaning forward. "I said, get out. I will not tolerate the way you acted to my wife."

"Y-your wife?"

Robert nodded, barely constraining his fury. "You and your wife are no longer welcome here. Good luck with finding another place to stay."

The man started sputtering but Robert was already moving toward the door, his heart in his throat. Alysse was likely devastated at what had just happened and he wanted to find her.

He needed to find her.

Taking two steps at a time, he hurried to her room, finding the door standing open. Alysse was standing by the bed, placing her things into her valise, her sobs filling the room. Robert's heart squeezed painfully in his chest as he stepped inside the room, clearing his throat so she would know he was there. "What are you doing?"

She stilled, keeping her back toward him. "I-I know you are going to ask me to leave. I'm saving you the conversation."

Robert stood his ground, though he wanted to reach out and take her into his arms. "What made you think that?"

She turned then, and he saw the tears coursing down her cheeks. "B-because... did you not hear what Stephen said?"

"I don't care what Stephen said," he ground out. "It doesn't matter."

She made a sound as she collapsed on the bed, holding a dress in her hands. "My father, he was arrested in Savannah. H-he stole money and was sent to prison for his crimes. My mother killed herself, unable to live with the shame of what he had done. I—have no one, no money, a tarnished name, and no future."

He stepped forward, crouching down in front of her before taking her shaking hands in his. He forced himself to meet her gaze, seeing the pain and anguish in their depths. She was stronger than he had originally given her credit for. "What if you took my last name?"

Her eyes widened. "W-what?"

Robert swallowed hard. "I don't want you to leave. I want you to stay. I don't care if your father is in prison nor do I care who you were before you came to me. This is the Alysse I care about, the one who has helped me turn this hotel around in a matter of days. I—I want this Alysse to be my wife."

"Robert," she breathed, tears flooding her eyes once more. "Are... are you certain?"

He nodded, the tightness in his chest growing steadily by the moment. If she didn't accept his proposal, he would lose her, and he would once again be lonely. After meeting her, he never wanted to be alone again. "I can't offer you a large home or fancy clothing, but I can offer you my affection for the rest of your days."

She sobbed and wrapped her arms around his neck, causing them both to end up on the floor with Alysse laying on top of him. Robert laughed as he hugged her close. "I asked them to leave."

She pulled back to look at him. "You did?"

He nodded, tucking a stray curl behind her hair. "I did. I would rather not have any guests at all than to have ones that were rude."

"He was my fiancé," she admitted, with a sigh. "And she was a close friend."

Now he understood her reaction. Careful not to send her to the floor, he helped them both to their feet, taking her hand in his. "Come."

"Where are we going?" she asked as he pulled her out of the room and down the stairs, paying no attention to the gasps of the couple that were walking out of the dining room at that very moment. Robert stopped and gave him a smile. "Would you be willing to be our witnesses for our wedding?"

"Robert!" Alysse started, tugging on his hand.

He ignored it, watching as the woman's gaze softened. She looked at her husband and they both nodded. "We would be honored to. My husband here, he is a preacher. He can perform the wedding now if you would like."

If that wasn't a sign, Robert didn't know what was. He looked over at Alysse, who had tears in her eyes and arched a brow. "What do you think?"

She gave him a soft smile. "I can't think of anything else I would rather do."

Robert squeezed her hand and turned back to the couple, their only remaining patrons of the hotel. "Well then, I guess we are asking for your assistance if you would be so kind."

The woman smiled and held out her hand to Alysse. "I'm Bertha Madden and this is my husband, Pete. We would like to tell you that your food is wonderful."

"Thank you," Alysse said, with a giggle.

Robert also shook the couple's hands before turning to his now fiancée. She looked beautiful and his heart squeezed with happiness as he thought of what they were about to do. "Shall we?"

She reached for his hands, tenderness in her eyes. "We shall."

"Well then!" Pete announced with a clap of his hands. "A wedding it is!"

Robert listened as the preacher started the wedding ceremony, losing himself in Alysse's eyes. The hotel could burn to the ground and they could lose all of their money, but as long as he had her by his side, that was all that mattered.

CHAPTER 15

*T*hree nights later, Alysse fidgeted with the lace on her sleeve as she watched the couples pour into the hotel, already losing count of how many had already arrived. In fact, she reckoned the entire town was in the dining room, sampling the food that she and Robert had already prepared. The musicians were playing a lively reel in the corner, and some couples were enjoying a dance in the cleared space at the back of the dining room.

All in all, it seemed that her tea party had worked.

She sighed and looked down at the battered gold band on her finger, a smile coming to her face. When Robert had presented the circle to her, he had told her that it had been in his family for generations and that every woman had worn the band. She knew he hadn't thought it was enough for her, but to Alysse, it was the most precious thing she owned.

Next to her husband that was.

Alysse's eyes scanned the crowd as she looked for her handsome husband, finding him talking to a small group of people who seemed enamored with his food. She was more than enamored by him, the man she was learning more and more about each day. He constantly surprised her and never in her life had Alysse felt more cared for as she did every time she was in Robert's arms.

She was happy, far happier than she had ever been.

Stepping into the room, she made her way to her husband's side, sliding her arm into his. "Good evening. I hope he is not telling you the particulars of how he prepared the food."

The group chuckled, and Robert slid his arm around her waist, pressing a kiss in her fragrant smelling hair. "Of course not, my darling wife. Why would I bore them like that?"

She looked up at him with a smile. "Because I know you and you enjoy talking about your food."

"And what a fine fare it is!"

They all turned to see the preacher walk through the door, a broad smile on his face. "I see that you finally took my advice my friend."

Robert chuckled, his own gold band glinting in the candlelight as they greeted the preacher. "I'm afraid to say that we don't need your services in that regard."

The preacher looked from Alysse to Robert, slowly shaking his head. "No, you do not. You make a fine couple and I am glad to see that you have found each other at last."

Alysse smiled as she leaned into Robert's touch. She was glad that she had found him as well.

Robert squeezed her waist before letting go, grabbing her hand instead. "Come," he said. "I wish to dance with my wife."

Alysse allowed him to lead her to the dancing space as the lone sound of the violin played a slow tune, sliding her hand in Robert's. He winked at her as they started to move along with the rest of the couples. "I confess, I have two left feet."

She laughed. "My feet can take the trampling on, I assure you. Do you think we were successful tonight?"

He nodded, his eyes sparkling with excitement. "I think the entire town has turned out for the party. If we are lucky, they will share the news and our hotel will become the premier stop for all weary travelers."

Alysse loved the sound of him referring to it as theirs together. She had so many plans for the hotel and they had already discussed the need for a tea party once a month so that the women could have a break from their day to day chores. Even tonight she had learned many a name, hoping that she could start to form lasting friendships within the town itself.

After all, this would be where they would raise their future children and grow old together.

He swung her around the room and she laughed, unable to help it. Here she was not judged by her past but would be for her future and her future was seemingly bright in the arms of her husband.

"You look happy," he murmured in her ear as they came back together.

"I am," she answered. "Unbelievably happy, dear husband."

Robert growled. "I do enjoy the sound of that."

"Then you better get used to it," she teased as the song came to an end. "Because I will say it until the day I take my last breath."

"You have no complaints from me, my darling wife."

~

The next few months, Alysse watched as their hotel grew to be one of the regular stops on the stagecoach route, meeting more people than she cared to mention. Robert's dining fare gathered attention from each patron that ate in their dining room and the little by little, the funds grew so that changes could be made with the hotel. She and Robert hired help in both the hotel and the kitchen and even purchased a small home not far from the hotel so that they could grow their own family.

One night, as she gazed up at the stars from their porch, Alysse whispered a prayer and a thank you to those above her, knowing they had taken the worst possible things that could happen to a person and turned it into something beautiful, something that she could not see herself living without. Her life might have been rich with earthly belongings once, but this life, it was rich with things that were far more precious.

~*~*~

Thank you so much for reading my book. I do hope you enjoyed reading about Alysse and Robert and their trials and tribulations in 'When Love Comes to Town'.

If you enjoyed reading this book may I suggest that you might also like to read my recent six book box set release 'When Love Comes Calling' next which is available on Amazon for just $0.99 or free with Kindle Unlimited.

<u>When Love Comes Calling - 6 Book Box Set</u>

~

The Making of Miss Ellen

Prologue

hicago, Illinois, 1865
        Ellen Howard poured herself another cup of tea, faking a smile as she did so for another member of Vera Richardson's social circle. She tried to be subtle as she glanced at the ornate mantel clock ticking time slowly away. The women would surely be there for another half hour at least and, as always, Ellen's benefactress would expect her to remain until the last guest had departed from the building.

"Mrs. Forrest has taken to ordering her silk from the dressmaker's catalogue," Mrs. Ivy Brown remarked.

"Do you mean to tell me she pays for it before it even arrives?" Vera asked, putting a gloved hand to her mouth in shock.

Mrs. Brown nodded, relishing her bit of news as she let the other ladies drink it in.

"I can't imagine doing that," another woman piped up, her lacy fan fluttering, blowing the tendrils of her curly auburn hair, which she was attempting to hold back with jeweled pins, placed around her cheeks and forehead. "You can't tell a single thing about quality from a *magazine*. I always thought that the out of town seamstress she is devoted to was quite questionable."

"Well, all I have to say is that she will find herself in a fix if she ends up with silk that is of poor and unworkable quality," Mrs. Brown commented. "You know, her daughter Mirabelle is of an age to be looking for a husband, if they buy material and then it turns out dreadful, she hardly has the money to invest in new silk and still have a seamstress make the dress. When a girl is in the circle of eligibility, it could surely prove to be a deadly mistake."

The other women clucked in agreement.

"She shouldn't risk jeopardizing Mirabelle's chances, of finding a beau," Vera stated. "A girl must be at her best to get a husband."

"Most certainly," Mrs. Brown replied. "Unfortunately, Mrs. Forrest's husband hasn't created the best foundation for his daughter. To be honest, her chances are damaged as it is." She took a sip of coffee, appearing thoughtful. "Some are fortunate to have good futures in mind for their girls though." She grinned at both women, assuring them that they were both included. Then her eyes landed on Ellen.

Ellen offered a brief smile before looking away, sipping her drink and hoping Mrs. Brown's attention wouldn't remain on her for too long. Although, she was having no such luck today.

"You must have exciting prospects in mind for Miss Ellen," Mrs. Brown aimed her remark at Vera.

"Oh, we do," Vera answered.

Ellen glanced over, silently asking what these prospects might be.

"Does Mark Brooks have anything to do with them?" Mrs. Brown asked, lowering her voice conspiratorially.

Vera lifted her chin, grinning. "Most certainly. I've spoken to the Brooks family and they are quite in agreement with the match."

The other women offered their congratulations while Ellen sat dumbfounded and feeling quite chilled to the bone.

Mark Brooks....it couldn't be. Ellen barely kept the chill that ran down her spine from becoming an audible shudder. Mark was certainly an eligible bachelor, no one could argue with that, but, the fact that he was the best catch in the city didn't mean he was a decent person. He was a lady's man, everyone knew that, but because of his position, no one seemed to care. He was present at every social gathering the Richardson's held. Ellen had despised him from the start. His inconsiderate remarks and haughty manner, which assured him he got whatever he wanted, even if it was by force, were utterly repulsive in her mind. She'd always pitied the woman who finally ended up with him. All the money in Chicago couldn't make up for the fact that a woman would be helplessly caught in his aggressive shadow for the rest of her life. It appeared that the woman she should have been pitying all along was herself.

"I'd advise you to count your blessings, Ellen," Mrs. Brown said, jabbing a finger in her direction. "It's not often a girl makes off with a catch like that. Your future is squared away which is a precious convenience at times like this."

Ellen's throat had constricted to the point of painfulness, but she managed a meek "Yes, Ma'am."

"Girls are having to go about finding husbands in the most unnatural of ways nowadays," Mrs. Brown said, obviously in no mood to get off her soap box just yet. "Did you know that girls are even accepting marriage proposals from men who advertise in the newspaper?"

"It's much like purchasing a horse, is it not?" Vera commented.

"Exactly. However, this is out West. It's not quite as surprising, when you consider that uncivilized corner of the world, that they would entertain such a thing. But, still. It's indecent if you ask me."

The other women agreed wholeheartedly while Ellen sat in silence, stewing her own whirling emotions.

Mark Brooks. God help her...

~*~*~

'When Love Comes Calling - 6 Book Box Set' is available on Amazon for just $0.99 or *FREE* with Kindle Unlimited simply by clicking on the link below.

Click Here for Your Copy of When Love Comes Calling - 6 Book Box Set

A NOTE FROM THE AUTHOR

Dear Reader,

Thank you for reading my stories.

The foremost reason that I love writing about the pioneering times of the West is that the lifestyle they had to endure is so vastly different compared to today's norm, yet with a simplicity and purity which in itself is so very refreshing.

I try to ensure that the story lines derived from these times are suitable for anyone and of any age.

Be sure to keep an eye out for the next book in this series which is coming soon.

Callie Gardner

Other books by Callie Gardner
  All available to download for *free* with **Kindle Unlimited**
  • Western Heart's Desire 4 Book Box Set
  • A Change of Heart
  • Home Is Where the Heart Is
  • The Doctor's Healing Heart
  • Love Grows in Crystal Creek

~

Newsletter

If you love reading sweet, clean, **Western Pioneer Romance** stories why not join Callie Gardner's newsletter and receive advance notification of new releases and more!

Simply sign up here: http://eepurl.com/cJoqqb

And get your *FREE* copy of **Maggie's Education**

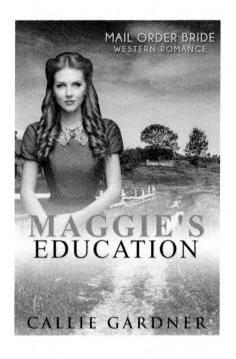

~

Contact Me

If you'd simply like to drop us a line you can contact us at **calliegardnerbooks@gmail.com**

You can also connect with me on my new Facebook Page
https://www.facebook.com/AuthorCallieGardner/

I will always let you know about new releases on my Facebook page, so it is worth liking that if you get the chance.

LIKE Callie's Facebook Page **HERE!**

I welcome your thoughts and would love to hear from you!

I will then also be able to let you know about new books coming out along with Amazon special deals etc

Printed in Great Britain
by Amazon

40700301R00040